MINI CLASSICS

CINDERELLA

A Parragon Book

Published by
Parragon Books,
Unit 13-17, Avonbridge Trading Estate,
Atlantic Road, Avonmouth, Bristol BS11 9QD.

Produced by
The Templar Company plc,
Pippbrook Mill, London Road, Dorking, Surrey RH4 1JE.

Copyright © 1994 Parragon Book Service Limited

All rights reserved.

Designed by Mark Kingsley-Monks

Printed and bound in Great Britain

ISBN 1-85813-660-1

MINI CLASSICS

CINDERELLA

RETOLD BY STEPHANIE LASLETT
ILLUSTRATED BY CAROLINE SHARPE

||| •PARRAGON• |||

Once upon a time there was a fine gentleman. He had a young daughter but sadly, his wife died and in time he married again. His new wife was proud and haughty. She had two daughters of her own who were exactly like her in all things. But the man's own daughter was sweet and good, just like her dear mother had been.

Gladly she welcomed her new relations, hoping they could all be friendly and live together happily — but it was not to be.

No sooner was the wedding
over than the stepmother
began to show herself in
her true colours.

She could not bear her
husband's pretty daughter
and made her do all the
housework. Every day she
made her wash the dishes,
scrub the tables, sweep the
floors and beat the rugs.

Her stepmother and stepsisters were waited on hand and foot and wanted for nothing. Each night the poor girl climbed the stairs to the very top of the old house and there she slept, curled up on a straw bed in the dusty attic. Her sisters had fine rooms, hung with beautiful silk curtains.

There they lay upon soft beds with perfumed pillows and satin coverlets.

Each had a large mirror on their bedroom wall so they might preen and admire themselves from head to foot. But their little stepsister never had time to look in a mirror. She was too busy washing dishes at the sink.

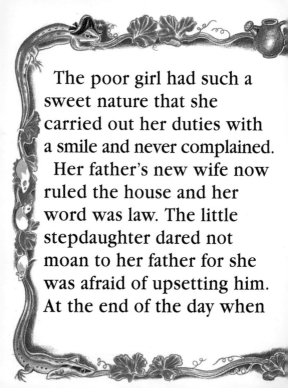

The poor girl had such a
sweet nature that she
carried out her duties with
a smile and never complained.
Her father's new wife now
ruled the house and her
word was law. The little
stepdaughter dared not
moan to her father for she
was afraid of upsetting him.
At the end of the day when

her work was done, the little girl would sit down near the warm cinders and ashes of the kitchen fire and dream of happier times.

When her stepmother saw her sitting there she laughed and called her Cinderwench, but soon her two stepsisters had given her a new name: they called her Cinderella.

But even though little Cinderella was dressed in rags and tatters, she was a hundred times prettier than her sisters in their beautiful gowns. They were so often in a bad temper, and pouted and sulked so regularly, that both their faces had grown quite ugly.

One day Cinderella found her two sisters in a state of great excitement.

"An invitation has arrived from the Palace!" cried one.

"The Prince is having a Grand Ball and we have been invited!" cried the other. Round the room they twirled, fluttering their fans and crowing with delight.

They ran to their bedrooms and pulled out gown after gown. "I shall wear my red velvet with the lace trimming and purple silk ribbons," cried the eldest. "And I shall wear my best gold frock with the diamond edging," said the youngest.

All day long they flounced before their mirrors in a

perfect agony of indecision.

"Which shall it be?" they sighed. "The pretty pink silk or the yellow brocade?"

Soon the floor was covered with clothes and poor Cinderella's heart sank, for it would certainly be she who would have to iron everything smooth once again.

Bright and early next day the two sisters left the house and went into town.

First they called on Mademoiselle de la Poche to discuss their make-up for the Ball. After endless dabbling in pots and gazing in mirrors, they finally left, laden with rouge, powder puffs and beauty patches.

Next they visited the wig-maker and chose new white wigs to wear with fat sausage curls. Smiling contentedly, they returned home, well pleased with their day's shopping.

The day of the Grand Ball finally arrived and the real preparations began. The sisters had not eaten a

thing for two whole days
to be sure that their waists
were as slim as possible.

"Cinderella!" they cried
from their bedchambers.
"Cinderella! Come and
help us dress!" And so poor
Cinderella was called hither
and thither as first one sister,
then the other demanded
help with their clothes.

"Tighter! Tighter!" they cried. And their stepsister pulled with all her strength upon the laces of their bodices but still their waists looked as large as ever.

Over a dozen laces were snapped and two fingernails broken before the sisters finally declared themselves satisfied with the results.

Not once did Cinderella complain. Indeed, she offered to help comb their wigs and the sisters accepted gladly, for her little fingers were more nimble than their own clumsy hands. Carefully they dusted rouge upon their cheeks as Cinderella looked on longingly.

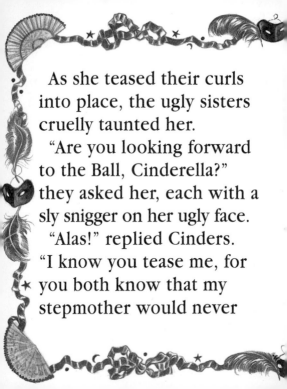

As she teased their curls into place, the ugly sisters cruelly taunted her.

"Are you looking forward to the Ball, Cinderella?" they asked her, each with a sly snigger on her ugly face.

"Alas!" replied Cinders. "I know you tease me, for you both know that my stepmother would never allow me to attend such a grand party."

"Ho, ho!" chortled the sisters. "How everyone would laugh to see such a Cinderella at the Ball. How they would admire your fine dress all tattered and torn! How they would envy your cinder-smudged shoes!" Poor Cinderella!

At last the ugly sisters had spent long enough in front of the mirror and decided they were quite perfect. It was time to leave for the Ball. Down the hall they flounced and Cinderella sadly watched them go.

When they had left the house Cinderella put her head in her hands and wept. Little did she know that her fairy godmother was listening.

"I do so wish that I could go to the Ball," sobbed Cinders. And no sooner had she finished speaking when her fairy godmother appeared before her.

"I am your fairy godmother Cinderella," said the kind fairy. "And I have come to grant you one wish. Do you wish with all your

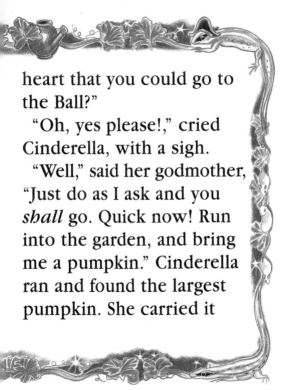

heart that you could go to
the Ball?"

"Oh, yes please!," cried
Cinderella, with a sigh.

"Well," said her godmother,
"Just do as I ask and you
shall go. Quick now! Run
into the garden, and bring
me a pumpkin." Cinderella
ran and found the largest
pumpkin. She carried it

back to her godmother, all
the while wondering how
this could possibly help.
Her godmother tapped it
with her magic wand and
the pumpkin was instantly
turned into a fine coach.

"Now fetch me six grey mice from the mouse-trap," ordered the fairy godmother.

One at a time, Cinders let the mice free and, as they ran squeaking from the trap, each was tapped with the magic wand. Soon six fine white horses stood proud and gleaming beside the golden coach.

"Now we need a fine coachman," declared the old woman. "I wonder what we might use?" Then Cinderella had an idea.

"I will go and look in the rat-trap," she said. "If there is a rat there, he may make a good coachman."

"What a good idea!," replied her godmother.

Cinderella brought the trap to her, and in it were three huge rats. The fairy inspected them all and finally chose the one with the longest tail.

She touched him with her magic wand and in a flash he was turned into a fat, jolly coachman with smart grey whiskers.

"Now for the footmen," smiled the godmother. "Go again into the garden and you will find six lizards behind the watering-pot. Bring them to me!"

Again the magic wand
flashed and the six green
lizards were turned into six
smart footmen. Each was
dressed in a smart green
uniform, all embroidered

with gold and silver thread, and splendid green hats now perched upon their heads. They bowed low to Cinders before jumping up behind the coach.

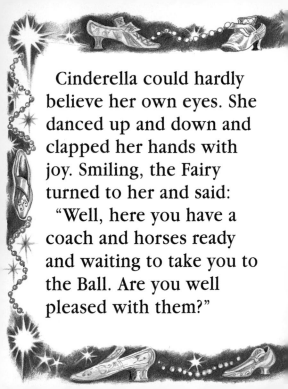

Cinderella could hardly believe her own eyes. She danced up and down and clapped her hands with joy. Smiling, the Fairy turned to her and said:

"Well, here you have a coach and horses ready and waiting to take you to the Ball. Are you well pleased with them?"

"Oh, yes!" cried Cinderella, "but I could not possibly go to a Ball dressed as I am in these horrid rags."

Once again her godmother waved her wand and, in an instant, Cinderella's tatters were turned into a lovely dress of silver and gold and sparkling glass slippers lay on the ground at her feet.

Cinderella's happiness was complete! But as she climbed into the coach, her fairy godmother warned her that she must be sure to leave the Ball before midnight, for if she stayed one moment longer, the coach would become a pumpkin again, her fine horses mice, her coachman a rat, her footmen lizards, and her clothes would change back into shabby rags once more.

With a happy smile and a wave, Cinderella promised her godmother that she would not forget. Then the coachman cracked his whip and she was on her way to the Palace.

When she arrived, the King's son was told that an important princess was waiting outside. He ran to welcome her and gave her his hand as she stepped down from the coach.

As the Prince led Cinderella into the hall, the musicians lowered their instruments and everyone stopped dancing to stare at the beautiful girl who gracefully descended the stairs on the arm of the Prince.

An excited hubbub broke
out amongst the guests.
"What an exquisite face!
Such beautiful hair! Who is
she? Who is she?" they cried.

The King and the Queen sat at the end of the hall. Murmuring with open admiration, the dancers parted as the Prince led his lovely new guest across the floor. When they drew near, the old King caught his breath. It was a long time since he had seen such beauty and grace.

As Cinderella passed her ugly sisters, she held her breath. Perhaps they would recognise her! But she had nothing to fear, for the sisters were so dazzled by the splendour of her dress that they saw nothing else.

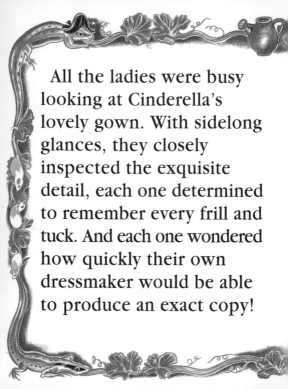

All the ladies were busy looking at Cinderella's lovely gown. With sidelong glances, they closely inspected the exquisite detail, each one determined to remember every frill and tuck. And each one wondered how quickly their own dressmaker would be able to produce an exact copy!

The Prince could not take his eyes off his sweet young companion and all the young ladies looked on enviously as the two of them slowly waltzed around the floor.

When supper was served, the Prince ate not a single morsel, so closely did he watch over Cinderella.

After the meal was over, Cinderella went and sat down by her sisters. With a kind smile she offered them oranges and lemons.

The ugly sisters were astonished by her attention and could only gawp, for they did not know this grand lady and they did not think that she knew them.

Then the dancing began again and, whispering sweet words, the Prince asked Cinders to be his partner.

The orchestra played a romantic waltz and the Prince held Cinderella tightly in his arms.

Cinderella was so happy
that she thought her heart
would burst. She closed her
eyes and silently thanked
the fairy godmother who
had made all this possible.

Suddenly her eyes opened
wide. She could hear the
clock striking midnight!
With a gasp, she broke
from the Prince's arms and

ran across the room. All
the guests stared after her
in amazement as she fled
up the stairs and out of the
Palace. Behind her the
chimes of the clock rang
out. One! Two! Three!
Four! Quickly she skipped
down the steps towards
her waiting coach and
horses. Five! Six! Seven!

Eight! Soon she would be dressed in rags! Faster she ran and in her haste one pretty glass slipper fell from her foot.

Fearful of the time, young Cinderella did not stay to collect her shoe but raced on down the stone steps. Nine! Ten! Eleven! rang out the clock and as she drew near to her coach she heard the final chime.

Twelve! It was midnight! Suddenly the fine gilt coach disappeared and there in its place stood a pumpkin with six mice, six lizards and a fine grey rat running nearby. Once more Cinderella was wearing her tattered old dress. Tightly clutching her one glass slipper, she quietly slipped away into the shadows.The other glass slipper lay gleaming on the stone steps.

Breathlessly, the Prince ran down the steps and turned to his guards.

"Did you see the princess leave?" he gasped.

But they had seen no-one but a poor country girl, all dressed in rags. Later that night the two ugly sisters returned home from the ball. Cinderella sat by the fire and yawned as they bustled into the room.

"What a long time you have been!" she cried as she pretended to rub the sleep from her eyes. With much fluttering of fans, her sisters recounted all that had happened at the Grand Ball. They described the unexpected arrival of a young princess, the most beautiful girl they had ever seen. Cinderella's eyes shone as they told her how the Prince had eyes only for her and danced with no-one else all evening.

"But she seemed to prefer our company," added her older sister with a superior smile and a toss of the head.

"Yes, indeed," agreed the younger sister. "She sat beside us and offered us oranges and lemons from her own hand." Cinderella hid a smile and asked if they knew her name. The sisters admitted that her identity remained a mystery and the only clue to her whereabouts was a pretty glass slipper left lying on the steps.

"The Prince is determined to find its owner," they told Cinderella in braying voices. "His mind is quite set on it."

This was indeed very true and a few days later the King's son issued a Royal Proclamation. He would search all the land until he found the girl whose foot exactly fitted the glass slipper, and then he would make her his bride.

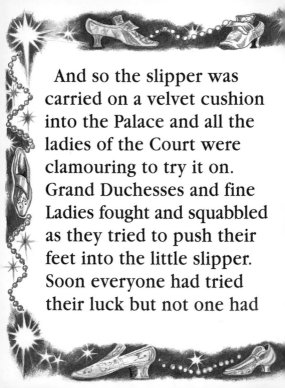

And so the slipper was carried on a velvet cushion into the Palace and all the ladies of the Court were clamouring to try it on. Grand Duchesses and fine Ladies fought and squabbled as they tried to push their feet into the little slipper. Soon everyone had tried their luck but not one had a foot dainty enough to fit inside the pretty shoe.

Then the Court footmen set off to visit all the grand houses throughout the country. Each young lady looked at the shoe and hoped for the best, but try as they might, their foot would not fit.

Soon the footmen arrived

at Cinderella's home. With loud cries of delight, the ugly sisters pulled the poor young men inside. Each was determined to make the little slipper fit. Grunting and groaning, they slowly squeezed their toes inside the fragile glass but at last, with moans of despair, they had to admit defeat.

Then the footmen spied
Cinderella and insisted she
try on the shoe. Her sisters
watched in disbelief as
Cinderella slipped it onto
her foot. It was a perfect fit!

Their astonishment grew
even greater when little
Cinderella put her hand in
her pocket and pulled forth
the other slipper. The Court
footmen bowed low before
her. This was the Prince's
bride! Then the fairy godmother appeared and in a
flash Cinderella was once
again dressed in her finery.

Now her two sisters could not fail to recognise the fine, beautiful lady whom they had seen at the ball. They threw themselves at her feet and begged to be forgiven for all the ill-treatment they had made her suffer. With a merry laugh, Cinderella drew them to their feet.

"Fear not, sisters," she said. "I am so happy that I can forgive you anything. I am to marry the Prince and wish everyone to share in my joy."

With tears of shame they hugged her and swore that from thenceforth they would try to follow her example and be as kind and as loving as she.

Her father and stepmother were soon sharing the good news and soon they were all on their way to the Palace.

The Prince was waiting for her on the steps and soon Cinderella was in his arms. He had found his true Princess at last.

The wedding took place the very next day as church bells rang out across the kingdom. Everyone rejoiced and made merry but none was as happy as Cinderella and her handsome Prince.

CHARLES PERRAULT

Cinderella first appeared in print in 1697 in a
collection of fairy stories written by the French
poet and storyteller, Charles Perrault (1628-1703).
The collection brought together many half-
forgotten traditional folk tales, including
Bluebeard, *Little Red Riding-Hood* and *Puss
in Boots* and together they became known as
Mother Goose's Tales. Written in a simple,
unaffected style, Perrault's stories quickly
became popular in France and later
throughout the world.

There has been considerable dispute over
the years as to the exact author of these tales
and some experts believe that it was actually
Perrault's son, Pierre (1678-1700) who
compiled and recorded the stories for posterity
when he was only 17 or 18 years old.